Holygrams

Subtitle: The Adventures and Misadventures of
Bobbin Robin.
Copyrighted
June 17th,2021

By Chris Briscoe.

Published by Chris Briscoe Publishers,June
17th, 2021.

Chapter One:

Robin and Wren Tie the Knot.

This is a tale of the adventures, exploits, and even mishaps of Robin Bovin whose nickname is Bobbin Robin. He acquired that name "Bobbin Robin" because he was known to be like a "bobbin robin"; a bobbin robin means a jumping robin; for those of you not acquainted with the beloved bird, robin, well, here in the U.K. the robin bird is beloved - certainly beloved in England enough to have been crowned as the National bird of England, which is called the European robin. Yet, some people have never met this little robin. For example, if you find yourself in South Korea where the people I spoke to have never heard or seen a robin because it hasn't flown that far east; so here's a picture of one; you can spot one as it's got a red breast - that's why his full name is Robin Redbreast.

This little fellow appears often on the front of Christmas cards.

Robin is so famous - even for the way it jumps, there's a song called, "When the Red, Red Robin Comes Bob-Bob-Bobbin' Along" first published in 1926.

But in this story, Robin was nicknamed Bobbin Robin for the way he spent his days and energies bobbing and weaving and ducking and diving trying to make more than a few "bob".

Robin Bovin, alias "Bobbin Robin", was married to his secondary school sweetheart, Jenny Wren, who he had first met in their elementary school-days. Since her family name is Wren, and her first name is Jennifer, it wasn't long before her parents started calling her "Jenny Wren".

The two of them - Jenny Wren and Robin Bobbin Bovin tied the knot one fine day in July, 1985. And the sequel to this was when "two little baby robins" appeared two years later from the same egg so that made them identical twin-boys.

Robin is a self-confessed entrepreneur who deals in anything which is selling like hot-cakes.

Bobbin Robin is something of what's called "a yuppy" which means "young, upwardly-mobile professional, i.e, "y.u.p.py" or "yuppy" as opposed to "hippy"; that word "yuppy" became a popular addition to our vernacular, i.e. our spoken English, during the 1980s when Margaret Thatcher was the British Prime Minister describing a person who was relying on his or own self-determination to advance him or herself in a spirit of enterprise and entrepreneurship which became a brand of Thatcherism under Margaret Thatcher; but later, that word became a label of derision or contempt for rich young individuals who had made a quick buck and were constantly greedy for more.

But for Robin, he didn't mind being called "a yuppy," in fact, he relished it as much as Margaret Thatcher being branded "The Iron Lady" by the Russians, even though, for them, it was probably a label of derision. Even Robin had signed himself up for one of the Mrs. Thatcher's Government scheme called, "The Enterprise Allowance Scheme" which was an initiative set up by Margaret Thatcher's Conservative Government which gave a guaranteed income of forty British pounds per week to unemployed people who set up their own business, which Robin had applied to and been a beneficiary when setting up his next enterprise.

His latest brain-child, for which his wife, Jenny Wren, calls "His worst brain-child.." to the point she said, "..I think it's worse than Dr.

Frankenstein's creation!"

Robin had been inspired with what he thought would be his best money-making scheme:

Tomb-stone holograms or what he called them "holygrams".

But since it's best to get it from the horse's mouth or robin's mouth, here's Bobin Robin:

"I wanna tell you about my latest invention which I seriously believe could be my ticket to a much better life, if I play my cards right, it may be my lucky break into the big-time!"

"See, one day, I was thinking hard, as I do. And I was thinking that so many people, every year leave this planet and the only remains they leave for their poor and bereft dear ones who remain down here, and the only connection they have with them in death is an impersonal, cold slab of stone and an 'oft' inscription. How many times have we watched the scene of some poor widow or widower visiting their loved one and speaking to a large lump of stone?"

"Well, this idea came to me: how about modernizing the concept of visiting your loved-one's gravestone by using technology to connect with them at another level through holograms – you know those laser-beams of light which can project an image of your loved-one as you step towards the gravestone and break a laser-beam?"

"I mean, how about letting the concept of visiting your loved-one's grave be updated and bring it into the twenty-first century where you can actually speak or even interact with your loved-one by a hologram instead of an impersonal slab of cold stone?"

"Now you may question me, 'How on Earth can we interact with our loved-ones who might be in heaven?,' Well, I'll come to that later."

"When I first thought of installing holograms to gravestones, it was like a bolt of inspiration from heaven! But then, a quantum-scientist friend of a friend suggested those holograms could be even cooler than that, if we were to team them up with the power of quantum mechanics - a form of teleporting from the other side through quantum-tunneling – quantum communication. Not that I'm an expert in quantum physics, but I was introduced to Professor Troy who I heard is the leading authority on the complexities of quantum physics; this new invention of holograms, I call 'holygrams', which might offer a way to actually make contact with those who live on other side."

"And I'm not talking about the suspect activity of 'spiritism' where dead spirits are summoned in such things as 'séances' which some people call 'spiritualism' , which I prefer to call 'spiritism'. Because there's nothing spiritual or Godly about trying to contact spirits who are roaming spirits that are not from the realm of heaven but from the underworld which Christians and Jews call the realm of the Devil or Satan; but what I'm talking about is a better way and doesn't involve calling dead and bad spirits in séances etc, which doesn't involving calling-up captured or evil spirits, which is actually forbidden in the Bible; which is outlawed as much as witchcraft because it is actually a form extreme rebellion against God because when we seek magical powers and enlightenment through dead-spirits rather than through God or his angels, it is going against the natural order which God has ordained - especially since such spirits are working for the wrong enterprise because they are employed by their boss - the Devil - as opposed to God's natural order; and the Devil takes capture those roaming spirits for his own evil agenda through fear - that's what is the Biblical and Judeo faiths believe i.e.

Jewish and Christian belief. I realize some people don't believe in the Devil, but that pleases him even more because when people deny his existence, the Devil can work even more effectively by stelf, because every wise strategist knows, the best way to win every battle, is 'KNOW THY ENEMY!'"

"I'm instead, referring to the most modern and cutting-edge science called quantum physics and quantum tunneling by use of a hologram."

"So I contacted this quantum scientist who was a friend of a friend called Professor Troy, and shared with him my idea, asking him if it would it be possible, first, before interacting with the forces of quantum, for him to install a three-dimensional hologram of our dearly, departed loved-one by fitting each gravestone with the latest state-of-art technology, so that each gravestone has its own hologram or set of holograms which could be beamed from a projector on the top of the tombstone, via a lens which comes alive by beaming in recorded time, a beam of light - a hologram of their image."

"Professor Troy said to me when he heard about the concept of gravestone holograms, 'How novel! Holograms of your loved-one, instead of speaking to the air.' Then before I put down the phone, he said to me, 'Give me a few days to think about it'."

"The following week he called me – I think on

Thursday - and said to me, 'Your idea is good, but if we were to interact with the power of quantum physics, then we might be able to actually communicate in real time with our loved-one'."

"Well, of course, my reaction was, 'How on Earth could you do that when you are talking about a physical entity making contact with a spiritual entity'?"

"He replied, 'It's never been done before, as there's always existed an unbridgeable gulf between life here, and the afterlife, but the field of quantum physics opens up to us scientists and the world so many new and, until now, closed opportunities.' He said. 'See quantum particles of waves or quantum waves move at such terrific speeds and without being constrained by our classical laws of physics, there may be a chance they can actually penetrate the after-life. If we were to actually make contact with our loved-ones through the technology of quantum-tunneling, then those four-dimensions would become five dimensions'.

"Of course, I didn't understand at the time what he was going on about, so I just said to him, 'Troy, Professor, I give you complete authority to do whatever you think would serve the human race, and more than that, serve God.' I had added the words, '..and more than that, serve God' because I believe that this universe shows so much complexity in perfect harmony, enough that it looks like there is the most intelligent super-being who has pre-programmed everything or super-tuned everything. I then said to Troy, 'All I ask is that you wouldn't blow yourself up or anyone else, including someone's deceased'!"

"Troy replied, 'Well, in that case, let's make this partnership a real business partnership – you will need my scientific expertise to make this work, and likewise, I will need your business expertise'."

"I thought for a few seconds. I felt I could trust the man on the other side of the line - in my spirit and inner-intuition that he was genuine and not out for his own opportunist and self-serving agenda. So I replied, 'Yes, I could draw up a working contract whereby we each take fifty percent of the profits, and if we really apply our brains and passion to this project, it could be a marriage made in heaven by bringing the blessings of Heaven down to the devastation of Earth, which would result in a hell-of-a-lot of pain and mourning turned into a heaven-of-a-lot of joy and healing for potentially millions'. I said."

"Troy replied, 'Yes, if what I will try, succeeds, by creating a quantum tunnel between Heaven and Earth, between this life and the afterlife, then that mere three-dimensional hologram image would become not only a four-dimensional image of three spacial dimensions of length, width, and height, and one time-dimension of time, but actually be a five dimensional hologram, by acquiring from the world of the fifth dimension light particles that penetrate into our fourth dimensional world projected via that hologram'."

"He finished our conversation with the words, 'I'll see what I can do'."

So that was Bobin Robin explaining what had happened.

And so, Robin asked Professor Troy to make the first hologram or the prototype of these grave holygrams, and after three months of research and experiments, finally, Professor Troy had perfected what Robin had envisioned; which was, from the gravestone there was a lens which projected an image of the deceased, which, once a sensor picked up the visitor, it was activated. But not only that but actually penetrated into the Fifth Dimension and the beyond dimensions - even to the trans-dimensional world - that is the metaphysical world of what oversees our physical, atomic world and subatomic world.

And through an ingenious series of laser beams which were connected to a memory-bank, they had the recordings of the height of every family member so that depending on who was visiting the gravestone, then either a pre-recorded hologram or a quantum hologram was projected from the gravestone's projector. If the son was visiting, then the mother's hologram was directed towards him with a message to her son, as the same for the daughter, and if the husband was visiting, the recording was designed for him. So each hologram appeared whenever the person visiting the grave breaks the laser-beam, when a sensor inside connected to a databank can sense whether the visitor is a family member, or if the visitor is a friend or acquaintance, and so the type of hologram that appears depends on the type of visitor.

Of course, what with Robin's vision and Troy's application of it, the two partners hoped that their invention would catch both the imagination as well as peoples' sentimentality. As for Robin, his business instincts were telling him that he was onto a winning formula since he knew the potent force of catching the masses' imagination and the even more potency of touching the very heart-strings of their sentimentalities.

And once Troy had telephoned Robin that finally he had constructed their prototype, he invited him to come over to his garden to test it with a recently erected gravestone. Troy had erected that tombstone in the corner of his garden, next to his compost heap he kept, which nowadays was permeating the strong odour of decomposing leaves.

Chapter Two:
The First Prototype Hologram - Pre-Holygram with Bill and Vi

So on a Saturday morning in autumn, while the smell of those decomposing leaves was still potent in the air, Troy showed Robin his 'baby'.

Robin accompanied Troy to his back-garden, to one corner where Troy had erected a gravestone.

"Robin, see, here, over here in the corner there is an erected gravestone." Troy pointed to a single gravestone which he had spent the previous afternoon's two hours digging its hole and lifting it into the hole with the help of his grown up son.

"Right Robin, imagine you and I are brothers and we are here to visit our mother's grave. Now let's just walk to our mother's grave."

Troy motioned with his hand to let Robin lead the way for a reason: he wanted Robin to break the infrared beam of light first. As Robin walked into that infrared beam of light and broke it, there appeared a hologram from Troy's actual mother, who he had recorded with his mother, who had kindly recorded for him even though she was not yet, 'pushing up the daisies'.

When the hologram appeared, Robin suddenly stopped himself in his tracks, as his face betrayed the feeling of being spellbound of the image and sound in front of him,

"Ello, Son, is that you, come to visit your ol' mom?" Came the voice from the grave.

Suddenly, Robin shouted excitedly, and thumping the air with victory then giving Troy a resounding pat on his white-coated back, while shouting,

"TROY, YOU'RE A GENIUS! ONLY A GENIUS CAN EXECUTE SUCH AN INGENIOUS IDEA!"

"Not at all!" Troy replied. "It takes a genius to think of such an idea."

"Holy Job..!" Robin added. "..These holograms will be a great source of comfort for mourners - I thought we would call them 'holygrams'."

But, Robin, remember I haven't yet had the more important breakthrough of quantum-tunnelling of opening up a tunnel between this life and the after-life. That comes next.

But it took all of a year for Troy to achieve a quantum breakthrough after so many failures and set-backs. And by that time, his dear mother, Violet, had passed to the other side. And before she had died, Troy had asked Violet, "Mother, could I ask you for a huge favour, which I believe you would be doing the human race a huge service - one for which you will go down in history as a great woman; although I already know you a great woman since you have always lived your life in service to mankind, especially me, and my family, and of course, Dad, whose name was Bill, bless his departed soul."

So, after spending a year on such a project, in Troy's spare time when he wasn't lecturing at his university, finally Professor Troy had found a breakthrough in his work with quantum physics.

So one day, Troy invited Robin to take a look at his new invention of quantum-tunneling between Heaven and Earth. One night, Robin paid another visit where Professor Troy showed him his new breakthrough.

In the darkest of night, again Troy took Robin outside and led him to his back-garden, to where, at a prime spot where during the day, there is the lushest grass and sun, he had built his own, with his son, Jonny, a really special mausoleum to his dearly departed mother and father, bless their souls, who he believed had been united since they were sincere, believing Christians.

This time Professor Troy led the way to his parent's mausoleum. He had erected a grand structure made out of marble and which had been specially sculpted into the shape of his parent's favourite destinations; for example, the sites of Italy including a gondola driven by a native wearing a striped shirt, in Venice, who was piloting the gondola with Troy's parents sitting inside - sculpted in more marble, arm-in-arm with wide-smiles and pure contentment, fixed for posterity.

As Troy and Robin approached the grand display, suddenly an invisible infra-red beam of light was broken by Troy, and the most beautiful holygram of his parents appeared - they were both waiting, arm-in-arm, sitting on something from the abode of Heaven, they had been evidently waiting for their son to appear. His father's voice could be heard first,

"There you are Son! Your mother and I have been waiting for you. So good of you to come again. You know your mother and I so do like it that you find time each night to visit us."

"Yes, we so do!" Concurred his mother, Violet, or 'Vi', to her friends and husband.

Bill could hardly contain he and his wife's excitement and contentment - pure joy, "You

know, Son, that your mother and I, here in Paradise, are everyday full of the perfect and abiding joy, peace, and contentment, enjoying gift after gift, of Christ's eternal gifts of fulfilled joy, and perfect peace, and real - the most tangible comfort; which we got a taste of when we roamed the Earth but now in Heaven, the joy and peace is actually so palatable - we can feel it physically every day - it's so thick you can actually cut if like a knife; when you enter this grand and huge throne-room and see the Lamb who was slain on his grand, golden and silver throne, who took our punishment on the cross, personally, so that we could be free of all accusation, therefore, dressed in his clothes of white, pure clothes, and worshipping him, our only reaction is to dance."
Explained Bill.

"And that's where and why we've been all day worshipping and dancing." Added Violet, with the broadest smile on her face, emanating pure joy and peace, and contentment

Violet continued as she also continued her broadest smile, "Yes, Troy, you know how your mom loves to dance. But our new bodies. WOW! My body and your dad's body are so much more agile here, and we can dance all day, if we want."

Suddenly Bill smiled and showed all his front canines, "AND THEY EVEN GAVE US EACH, ALSO, A BRAND NEW SET OF TEETH! NO MORE HORRIBLE, SMELLY DENTURES TO CLEAN EVERY NIGHT!" He proclaimed with a smile almost as big as his wife's, when she was talking about her cherished dancing with Bill and the blessed Lamb.

"WOW!" Troy responded with surprise. "DAD! YOUR NEW PEARLIES ARE SHINING WITH SUCH BRILLIANCE! YOU LOOK LIKE ONE OF THOSE MODELS ON A NEW TOOTHPASTE ADVERT!"

"YES!" Replied Bill. "I would have you to know that these, here pearlies adorning my mouth are whiter than the pearly gates in Heaven, but not more beautiful because they are made with turquoise pearl! But, I would have you know that these gritters are no way near the white and brilliant and pure and innocent, white brilliance of the innocent Lamb, Jesus Christ, whose wounds he bore for each of us, and still carries, for us all, individually."

"Yes!" Concurred Violet. "And what is more, you can still see those horrid but glorified wounds in Heaven in the glorified body of Jesus Christ - I saw them, up and close, when I went up close to Jesus when he embraced me with the strongest love, while his eyes were burning with the deepest, purest and strongest love; I spotted in his hands and feet, those scar-wounds, nail-pierced-wounds in the palm of his hands and the souls of his feet, embedded with beautiful, red-blood rubies!" Explained Violet.

After thinking deeply, Vi added, "Which makes us dance and worship even more!"

Bill added. "Which today we did, continually, with pure and grateful joy in our hearts. And what's more is, all of our faculties are in prim and pristine condition, never again going downhill because we will never age again! Isn't that great, huh!?"

Violet, suddenly had a deep, worried look on her face, which was so beautiful and young looking just a moment ago, "But we employ you to warn your dearest Penny, and your dearest Jonny, that if they haven't applied the cross and Jesus' blood - the innocent, pure, and spotless Lamb of God - to their hearts - their fallen spirits - which they and everyone inherited from the fall of mankind when Adam and Eve rebelled against God - the Lamb sacrificed to take their own punishment for every wrong-word or motive, which everyone cannot help committing, then their future would not have been sealed by God in his blood and the Spirit of God, but sealed by the devil in hell, suffering eternal torment and pain, forever! Which we can never imagine or consider for any of us - WHAT A GHASTLY AND DISASTEROUS OUTCOME, WHICH CAN EASILY BE AVERTED BY ONE DECISION OF RECEIVING JESUS INTO YOUR HEART AND FOLLOWING HIM FOR THE REMAINDER OF YOUR LIFE!" Appealed Violet, passionately.

"Yes! Please warn them before it's too late!" Concurred Troy's father.

"Yes, but today, your dad and I have had such a wonderful exercise, dancing all day. And here in Heaven, it's so cool, you don't need air-conditioning, and also, you don't need a heater because there's no cold weather, as there's no longer any seasons." Violet said.

"And neither is there any sea, anymore.." Added Bill .."But that doesn't mean your mom and I cannot enjoy those gondola rides in Venice, because here in Heaven you can do whatever you heart's desire, as long as the activity doesn't hurt anyone and is consented by each other."

Bill then added, "Yes! So your mom and I visited Venice last week, when we were both more contented than these two marble structures, enjoying again gondola rides, followed by a week of exploring Italy - staying at the best hotels, with silk sheets and silk pillow-covers - only the best for paradise-dwellers from Heaven!"

Just then, Violet put her arm of Bill, "Oh Bill, you remember, tonight, we are having another lavish, sixteen-course, double-banquet with the Lamb?"

"Oh, Yes!" Exclaimed Bill. "Jesus Christ personally invited us both with his deep, loving and impassioned words - He said, 'Bill and Violet, you will both be joining me for the my own Marriage Supper?' WOW! Just think, I we will be able to enjoy food which are full of the most jam-packed new and exotic flavour- even no where to be experienced on Earth but only in Heaven! Food which I have never tasted of before - and without my dentures, and now with these new pearlies, I will.., no, we will, so enjoy! Of the most exotic food and recipes from all over the different, various universes!" He said with excitement and anticipation.

"Violet squeezed Bill's arm, We'd better go, Bill." Beckoned Violet to leave for their blessed and delicious, and flavour-packed divine-appointment

"Yes, we better fly!" Bill exclaimed. And with that, they both blew kisses, and flew away in the dead of night - whisked away by the love of the Lamb calling them to his most wonderful and delicious Marriage Supper of the Lamb. And suddenly, their holygram disappeared.

And just Troy was left with Robin - with Robin,

initially speechless, looking upwards, with his eyes wide open, and his mouth wider open, looking gormless - muted in all his senses.

"WOOOOOW! ALL I CAN SAY, TROY, PROFESSOR, SIR, IS WOW! WOW! ISN'T GOD GOOD AND THAT LAMB. WHAT A HERO!" He responded as best he could in the circumstances.

Troy completely concurred. "And doesn't that marriage supper sound so delicious and scrumptious, my blessed folks talked about?"

Therefore, for Troy and Robin, their next challenge was to find a real life deceased, if you know what I mean. And because of the sensitivity of a loved-one dying, Robin and Troy had to tread very carefully so that they didn't upset anyone, not the least the one who is "pushing up the daisies", if you know what I mean.

And then, tragically for one family called the Truffles who have lived in Scunthorpe for seven generations, the matriarch of the family, a much beloved, Mrs. Ethel Truffle, passed away one night in her sleep. Leaving her husband of forty-five years along with their two grown-up boys, Tommy and Peter, to somehow make sense of it all.

Professor Troy was the first to hear about the Truffles' loss through the local newspaper. So after reading about their case, Troy telephoned Robin when they discussed whether this might be an opportunity.

Robin suggested that they offer the Truffles family the opportunity to be the first to try out the holygram gravestones services on a three months free-trial. Troy agreed it would be prudent to offer the first three month's trial-period free since this technology was both new technologically as well as culturally new; especially since the holygrams were still in the experimental stages; Robin suggested he could send them a letter, introducing himself as the CEO of 'Holygram Gravestones', offering them a free-trial of three months to try out the hologram. But Troy thought it would be more sensitive and less spammy if he wrote to the Truffles, himself, first introducing himself, and then Robin, along with his technology. Actually, one of Troy's friends had known the Truffles and Ethel Truffles' children from their school years. So sensitively, he sent them a letter introducing his business acquaintance Robin, along with this new technology offering a three month free-trial. He explained to them in the letter about this new technology he and Robin Bovin had invented, informing them that he thought it might be interesting for them and could in the future be a strong source of comfort and encouragement in their mourning period.

After a few days of considering this proposition, Ethel's husband, Arthur, thought that this new technology could be a great source of comfort for both him and his family.

So he signed up for a three-month trial-period. Then, Robin and Troy swung into action. And what is astounding is through Professor Troy's ingenious invention of connecting the power of quantum-tunneling with holograms to make holygrams, Ethel was able to be contacted and persuaded to beam messages from Heaven itself! From where she said in her first message beamed to Professor,

"WOW! Here in heaven, it is far beyond all you can imagine!" Ethel stated, enthusiastically. And what is more, you don't need faith anymore to draw near to God - you can see Him with your eyes. Do you remember reading in the Bible or have you ever read in the Bible, 'Without faith, it is impossible to please God?' Well, here in heaven, instead you can please him with love, with praise and worship, and adoration, which he loves us to do, his beloved children…" Ethel said. "..Actually, before coming to Heaven, I had always wondered why Jesus had his two favorite disciples, John and Peter, who alone Jesus had taken them up the mountain where they had met Moses, and all their body's were transfigured or reflected the whitest gleaming colour. But in Heaven I had asked Jesus why he had let John lean on his breast. Jesus replied that he would have let any of his disciples lean on his breast, if only they had asked him, or initiated that exchange."

Even though Ethel had departed this Earth last Wednesday in her sleep, and who had already been dead almost a week, through this new technology, Professor Troy was able to send messages to her, as well as receive messages from her.

So next, Troy and a few of our helpers installed the new technology of holograms into Ethel's gravestone. The first real holygram gravestone to be installed.

Chapter Three:

Arthur Pays His First Visit to Ethel's Grave - the First Gravestone with a Holygram

The day after Ethel had been buried, early the

next day, before his two sons, Tommy and Peter, had awakened, Ethel's husband, Arthur, left his house to visit her graveside for the first time since burying her.

As he approached Ethel's head-stone, Arthur actually didn't want to be at a graveyard when the sun was still not up, so the dark, eerie feeling he always hated at such places was compounded by his trepidation of thinking when will that hologram of his wife appear. As soon as his body broke that invisible laser beam, a holygram appeared of Ethel.

Arthur was so startled by the sudden appearance of Ethel since she looked so life-like; Robin felt he was now looking at a ghost so he did a sharp U-turn and began to head back; but then he heard his wife's voice and turned back to see her vision.

Ethel shouted after him, "Arthur, are you a man or a mouse? This is your ol' gal, Ethel. Come back here!" Ethel called after Arthur.

Arthur was actually doubly surprised because the hologram of Ethel was of a much more youthful and so now a spritely looking Ethel, of her former twenty year younger fifty-something self, much younger and with much less lines and burrows in her face. Which Arthur had noticed.

Arthur looked back at the image he had thought was a ghost and said, with his heart beating, "IS

THAT YOU, MY E, E,……ETHEL?"

Arthur shouted when he recognised his darling Ethel, "WOW! YOU CERTAINLY LOOK BETTER - THEY MUST BE FEEDING YOU WELL UP THERE!" He said.

Suddenly, Arthur was stunned to hear his much beloved wife of forty-five years answer him back, and what's more, in real-time.

Arthur was so shocked he shouted "Eeeeeeeeeeeeek!"

Ethel responded, "OF COURSE, IT'S ME! WHO

ELSE DO YOU THINK YOU WOULD FIND AT THE TOMB OF ETHEL TRUFFLE, YOU DAFTY?"

"Well, it's n..., n...,n..., not someone I was expecting to find – I m..., m...,m.....,m..., mean you don't usually expect to meet your deceased spouse fully a..,..a..,..a.., animated. Usually, what you find is just a cold slab of stone and a hole filled with your cold body!"

Ethel absolutely did not concur with her husband and replied, indignantly, "DON'T FOR A SECOND THINK THAT I AM LAYING HERE LIKE PIECE OF COLD, RAW BUTCHER'S MEAT GIVING UP,THE GHOST FOR SOME UGLY, DIRTY WORMS!" She shouted emphatically.

Ethel added, "NO! You can be rest assured that my body is still very warm - in fact it's never been warmer and my mind has never been sharper, as well as my eyes, ears and all my faculties, and that my joints and my body have become both supersonic and glorified, so I have never had such a good body and organs to go with it!" Ethel demonstrated this by showing Arthur the way she could move all her joints which only a few days ago were more ceased-up than an old farmer's tractor kept in storage for years – suddenly, Ethel started running on the spot – much to the envy of Arthur who went nearly as green with envy as one of the green ivy-plants which Arthur had planted at the foot of Ethel's grave.

"WOW! ETHEL MY DEAR, YOU REMIND ME OF THAT OLD T.V. SERIES FROM THE EIGHTIES,

SUPER-GRANNY, WITHOUT THE SCOTTISH ACCENT." Arthur shouted, amazed by his darling wife's transformation in the space of a week.

Ethel obviously wasn't amused as he was, as she stopped her demonstration of her new and agile body, and instead replied with a large dollop of indignation and repugnance, with the same volume as Arthur had used, "WE ARE NOT AMUSED!" She exclaimed.

"Oh, Ethel, you are surprising me! Not only that you are alive, but just how nimble you have become after one week in Heaven. WOW! Imagine what you will be like after six months there!" Arthur exclaimed.

Arthur's face was still white with fright, pinching himself that he was talking to his dead missus from the grave - that she had somehow overcome the grave.

Arthur decided to overcome his initial fear and take a closer look at Ethel. As he did, his reaction was, "WOW! Ethel, Dear, you don't look a day over fifty!"

"Well, I think it may have something to do with the good food they serve here..." Ethel replied. "..It's better than what they're serving at the Ritz or the Savoy - way better! Oh, Arthur, Heaven is way better than the Savoy Hotel, London, the food is way better! And only they have great and most comforting experiences while warning that those who have not washed their robes in the Lamb's blood have to suffer the flames of eternal hell and damnation."

"And there's not a crossed word said, anytime..." Ethel added. "..neither any lie, nor any common garden annoyance because here you can choose to do whatever you want within the boundaries of good morality. I actually went deep-sea diving the other day, actually here it one long day, there no concept of time or tomorrow or yesterday, and there's no need for the light of the sun by day or the light of the moon by night because, since the boss who is called the Lamb lives with us, constantly, he lives in such an amazing bright light, we don't need those temporary lights anymore because we now have the eternal light always with us. Actually, let me tell you, I've been living in Heaven for over a week now, but not once have I seen a clock on the wall or anyone wearing a watch - and do you know why? That's why I can't say yesterday because, up here, there's no time." She stated.

Arthur responded with a relieved smile, "WOW! It certainly looks like Heaven is doing you a world of good! Eth, love!"

"Well, I mustn't complain, Arthur! Actually, here, there's nothing to complain about!" Ethel stated.

"WOW! You look better than when you came back after two weeks in Torbay, Dear!" Arthur exclaimed, then walking up to the image in front of him, to get a better look, his reaction was, "HA!"

"WOW! This technology is grand, in it something Ethel? Isn't it marvelous what technology can do these days – even to overcome the grave, eh, Ethel, Dear?"

Ethel snapped back, "ARTHUR TRUFFLES, DON'T THINK FOR ONE SECOND IT'S BECAUSE OF THIS HERE TECHNOLOGY THAT I STAND BEFORE YOU TODAY, NOT COLD-BLOODED BUT HOT-BLOODIED WITH ALL MY FACULTIES GLORIFIED. IT'S MORE THAN MERE PHYSICAL CONSIDERATIONS THAT YOUR LOVING ETHEL HAS BEEN GIVEN A NEW AND ETERNAL LEASE OF LIFE AND

BEEN RE-ENDOWED WITH A FACE OF PRE-THIRTY YEARS!"

"YES, ETHEL, LOVE, I CAN SEE YOUR NEW BODY IS MUCH MORE ATTRACTIVE AND ATTRACTABLE!" Arthur said, looking over his wife's newly acquired, younger and much more sprightly body. "I must confess I was expecting that by now a brigade of worms had made off with you, my Dear."

"OVER MY DEAD BODY!" Replied Ethel. "AND WHAT'S MORE IS, MY BODY IS MORE RETRACTABLE CAUSE I CAN NOW MOVE IT IN ANY DIRECTION I WANT IT TO GO." Stated Ethel, confidently. "ARTHUR TRUFFLES, YOU'D BETTER BE WARNED THAT MY EYES ARE

BETTER THAN A BALD 'EADED EAGLE, SO DON'T THINK YOU CAN PAY ANY MORE OF YOUR VISITS TO SCUNTHORPE'S BOOKIES! I'VE GOT MY EYES ON YOU - WELL, AT LEAST ONE EYE."

"WHAT! All the time, my dear?" Asked Arthur.

"I MIGHT 'AVE!" Replied Ethel, feeling cagey with the whole truth.

Arthur gulped, and under his breath said, "I was wondering how long my freedom and winning-streak was going to last!"

Suddenly, Ethel screwed up her face and her countenance changed into a scary, nagging wife. "ARTHUR TRUFFLES, YOU HAVE BEEN TO THAT BOOKMAKERS, HAVEN'T YOU, IN MY ABSENCE? BUT NOW I CAN SEE ALL YOU DO, AND WOE AND BETIDE YOU IF I CATCH YOU PAYING ANOTHER VISIT TO THOSE BOOKIES..!" Ethel shouted in such a piercing shrill that even the elderly eighty-eight grounds-man turned around to look away from the bush of red and white roses he was pruning.

Then with a lower tone, she said. "And here's me thinking that my Arthur loved me so much, that he would wait at least a year before frequenting such a place of disrepute!"

"Oh, Ethel, Lovey, please calm yourself. I can see Heaven is doing you a world of good, please don't trouble yourself with mere earthly matters." Arthur tried to put Ethel's mind at rest.

"Yes, I can never complain because it's paradise here, much better than the Britain of the 2020s. It's one big praise party here!" Ethel said. "People call this place 'the afterlife' but now I know that the proper name is real life or eternal life because here, anything of real life and joy and peace is connected with our relationship with Jesus. Now I know why Jesus said the words when he prayed to his father, 'Now this is eternal life: that they may know you, the only true sovereign God, and Jesus Christ, whom you have sent.' Cause Arthur, I can say that this here is really living! And the most important message I can send to you, is you wouldn't want to miss out on this, and Hell is worse then what you have ever imagined!"

"But Arthur, please listen, because I have something important to tell you. Up here is a very special place, and we don't let any riff-raff come in, it's only for those who have washed their clothes in the Lamb's blood, whose clothes have been washed like bleach. So you must make sure you have washed yourself clean." Ethel cautioned Arthur.

"You know Ethel, I always have a bath at least once a week." Responded Arthur.

"No! I'm not talking about that," Replied Ethel.

"See the Bible says, that in heaven there are only those who wear the clothes or are given the white clothes of Jesus." Responded Ethel, who Arthur noticed was looking so healthy, including spiritual health through the infilling and communion with God, himself living in him, through his Holy Spirit.

"Oh Ethel. You don't need to worry in that department either." Arthur said, "I'm still using that whitener you used to use for my clothes." Replied Arthur.

"I mean here everyone wears clothes which are dazzling!" Responded Ethel.

Arthur replied, "Well, I don't think you will have

any complaints because I use that whitener you left me to use in our laundry room or utility room, Eth'."

"And regards my body hygiene, Ethel, I have been taking a bath, every day, as you always asked me along with my clothes." Arthur said, trying to convey his honesty.

"No, I'm not talking about that!" Ethel replied. "I'm talking about, in order for you to be accepted into Heaven, you need to confess that inside your heart there is a problem - it's actually the source or root problem of why you end up at the bookies once a week or whenever you succumb to your inner weakness; because your problem, Arthur, or the heart of your problem is the problem of the human heart, which can only be overcome by you coming to the cross and crucifying your old self with all its vulnerabilities; then allowing Jesus Christ's resurrected power to come into your life, by faith in the risen Lord Jesus, which is a tangible power in your life by the power of the Holy Spirit; so that, after you acknowledge that Jesus died on the cross and took your punishment for all your mistakes, then you can receive Jesus into your heart; then his Holy Spirit will come and make you into a brand, new person, with a new spirit and newness of life, with the power of God's Spirit working and abiding in you, In that case, then you will be accepted in Heaven with a rich welcome, Arthur." Explained Ethel. "But for that to happen, you must acknowledge that you are a sinner, I mean, that you have sin in your heart which you need to confess and repent of, and decide to not engage in, ever again!" Ethel added.

Arthur responded, "Hmmmnn, you will have to let me chew that one over, Ethel, Dear, with my cup of tea and a chocolate éclair, later on."

"As long as you don't chew on your pipe while I'm gone. Arthur Truffles, I'm watching you, don't think for one minute while the cats away, the mouse will play." Warned Ethel.

Arthur gulped again, as he placed his index finger inside the tiny space between his collar and neck to give it some air from the cool of the evening, as he felt hot under the collar. "Well, Ethel, my honey-pot, I had been thinking such thoughts since you left, and to be honest with you, I had felt tempted to not only chew on my tobacco but light it, and even light a cigar or two."

"ARTHUR TRUFFLES, DON'T EVEN THINK ABOUT IT!" Ethel's started shouting again as she did when her emotion took over.

Arthur gave another "guuuuulp," this time a much bigger gulp.

"But anyway, Arthur, Love, thanks for your honesty." Then after a few seconds of thinking, she reminded him, "Just don't let me catch you going anywhere near your pipe, anyway, I threw it away last year, along with your cigars, because none of them will do you, nor the house any good!" Ethel exclaimed. She started shouting out what she felt inside her emotion, "YOU REMEMBER HOW MUCH YOUR DIRTY SMOKING WAS RUINING MY NEW, WHITE SUITE WITH A YELLOW NICOTINE COLOUR AND MAKING IT SMELL THE PLACE OUT AND LEAVING THAT 'ORRIBLE RING ABOVE YOUR SEAT, AND OF COURSE, IT WAS DOING YOUR LUNGS AND MINE A HELL OF A DAMAGE! I heard from doctors that every time someone lights up they are taking a full eight minutes of your life." Ethel added.

Arthur wanted to get his wife off the subject of his cigars and gambling "Ethel, Dear, please calm yourself. What exactly have you been doing with yourself?" He asked Ethel.

Ethel replied, "Well, I have really enjoyed praising and worshiping the Lamb in the middle of this huge throng of people who each are wearing white clothes cleaned by the blood of the Lamb."

"I can imagine, it's one big praise party to God, everyday, every hour, isn't it?" Asked Arthur.

"Oh, yes, but we can do so much more than praising and worshipping, actually all those hundreds of things or activities I had on my bucket-list which I never got round to experiencing, well in Heaven, you can do what you want, go anywhere you want, even explore the universe by flying on your own because you can fly anywhere to explore; or doing any activity, like a scuba-diving or also, I have done paragliding, but the water in Heaven is so pure and clean and full and sweet to the taste, and the fish so friendly, as are all the animals of heaven, even the most ferocious, even in Heaven the Lamb can sit down and be friends with the lion, even the most ferocious shark and crocodile is friendly and docile." She said.

"What! Ethel, really, that's all you do is praise the big Man-God?" Asked Arthur, curious at Ethel's new home.

"No, of course not!" Stated Ethel. "Here, I can do all kinds of activities I have always wanted to do but couldn't because I lacked either the body of health or the courage to do such as para-gliding or parascending. Only the other day, I tried my hand at water-skiing. See, here when you arrive, you are given a new body of health and a face full of health when you were at your peak down here."

"WOW! I can't wait to join you there. And to receive a new body and my best face and body." Responded Arthur.

"Arthur, stop right there. I need to tell you something, actually warn you - about something: Since spending a week here, I have learned that between Heaven and Earth, there is a huge gulf or abyss that nobody can cross. You cannot come here, and in the same way, I cannot come there - well, until now, albeit, in the form of an image sent from here to there, that is. But what I need to warn you about is, even though I can only come to you through these holograms, well, once a person ends up, to their horror, in the most horrific place called 'Hell' then the gap between Hell and Heaven is absolutely unbridgable intractable without Jesus Christ living in your heart by the Holy Spirit."

"I am not. Arthur, don't even think I am for a minute." Replied Ethel. "Please, don't even think I am now up here as ancient as you, cause up here we have the privilege among a host of other privileges and the host of angels to be in our best self - I mean, here in Heaven, everyone is at their peak of what they were on Earth, meaning everyone is their best version of themselves - even Jesus Christ is the best version of himself - in his resurrected body with even the deep wounded scars of those nail-pierced scars driven into his hands and feet when he died for us. Thank the dear Lord, we don't have to bring with us the old, wrinkled and decrepit body we were when we left the Earth, so please show some respect for the deceased'.

Ethel paused, then suddenly thought deeply again. "Arthur, I have something to tell you, so please keep quiet for a few seconds, saying, or exclaiming, Is that Arthur, love? I know it's you, cause I can sense you now with this sensor which is even better than my senses I had when I was living on Earth. How uncanny is that - eh?" Ethel said, with a tone in her voice of a welcomed surprise.

She continued, "It's amazing these days technology, isn't it Arthur? And I want to say, Arthur, don't come here too often, Dear. I 'll let you come here every day for the first six months since you miss me so much your love and honey-pot, but after that you have to just snap out of moping around and try and get another activity into you okay. See, you still got Tommy and Peter to look after, and what is more, they need their father at home to cook them 'bangers and mash' or "egg and chips" when they get peckish, so hurry on home and enjoy the sense of freedom you have now that I am not around breathing down your neck and checking on you."

"But two or three activities I still forbid: Woe and betide you, Arthur Truffles, if I catch you or hear that you are frequenting the local bookmakers again and wasting our money, now that I have kicked the bucket!" Ethel warned Arthur.

"This business of holygrams, you can prepare as many holograms as you need, up to twenty of what you think is needed. And so, if I catch you, I will make sure that my next message which has some blue atmosphere in it is published when you have the gall to show your cheeky face here after showing your face in such places of disrepute as a bookies." Looking at Arthur more closely to check he was concentrating on her words, "You hear me, Arthur?" Boomed Ethel.

The closer Ethel got to him, the more Arthur's face showed an expression of amazement mixed with deep disbelief, as he wondered to himself if he had been at the bottle tonight.

"Yes, Lovey,.." He responded, "..Even though you're millions of miles up there, I still hear you and actually I am actually enjoying your nagging me from the grave because actually I miss you so much, I even miss your nagging! Would you believe it - I never thought I would ever say that - that I actually missed your nagging, like missing a dripping tap. But I do, Ethel, dear, that's how much I love you." As Arthur offloaded his confession, he noticed a single tear trickle down his cheek."

That was Arthur's first visit to his dearly beloved wife, Ethel.

Now that the holygram's prototype had been thoroughly assembled and tested, the next project was to hunt around for a way to fully automate or construct them in a mass-production way, as Robin's ambition was to mass produce them, either though flat-packs which could be assembled by someone with minimum digital or electrical expertise or through a person's minimal intuition; so they looked round for a suitable mass producer.

So Robin's and Troy's holygrams started out as one, and then two orders, and then, one week four, and then, as word of mouth spread locally, and bereaved families raved over the novelty and comfort of experiencing and even interacting with their cut-off loved-one, it began to sell better than hotcakes, because, as everyone knows, there's money in life as well as death, i.e. a hairdresser will never go out of business as much as a caretaker as people will always need burying or burning.

Chapter Four:

More Than A Voice From the Grave.

Arthur, at first, really appreciated the opportunity to interact with his deceased wife through these pop-up holograms. It was very novel and it gave him much comfort in his loss.

Arthur wrote in his dairy of his feelings and thoughts of the first week when for every day in the evening he paid a visit to his wife's side.

He wrote, *"I must say, this hologram technology is rather giving me a lot of comfort - much better than just a cold, slab of marble, it means I get to feel again the actual sense that Ethel is actually there with me talking with me from the grave which after she died, I really pined for.”*

He wrote the next evening in his diary entry, *“It felt weird this evening when I said to my Son, 'Tommy, Just going to mom's grave to pay respects. Hold the fort, here!' because thanks to this hologram technology, I do much more than pay my respects or lay a flower and a tear. I am actually confronted with her four-dimensional image where I feel like she is speaking to me in real time speaking from the grave.”*

But after two weeks of experiencing this and her strong rebuke or warning not to think that now he was free from her shadow that he could do what he wanted.

Well, before Ethel had died she had arranged with her lawyer or solicitor will where she has written a will to release her own personal savings and she had willed that her husband of forty five years receive £ 50,000 which he used £ 30,000 of that large sum of money to buy his dream-car of a British-racing-driver green jaguar Mark 4. But when Ethel got wind that he had spent her money or most of her money on a mere car, she was at first shocked, then appalled so much that she sent him a real-time hologram through Professor Troy quantum technology and this is what she said.

Professor Troy was a quantum scientist by trade

and so he had one day thought of one way to contact the dead using quantum tunneling technology. So he visited Ethel's grave one day and tried it out for himself and he found that it worked so well his laboratory-assistant had become so spooked by actually contacting Ethel, he had run away.

While Professor Troy was sufficiently built that he could hold onto his wits and courage and mind. But much to his relief and sense of excitement, his idea and invention worked and so he decided to re-program or install the second generation of holograms into Ethel's grave memory-bank which were actually messages sent and received from heaven population and he managed to contact Ethel herself and show her or inform her that her husband had bought or spent 30,000 pounds of his will from her on a brand new Jaguar Mark 4.

The message that came back hid her incandescent outrage that she kept inside her until Troy gave her the opportunity to pre-record a new message where she could air her incandescence or indignance. Her incandescence or her fury or GRAVE INDIGNANCE.

As Arthur climbed out his brand new Jaguar after stroking and smelling the chestnut dash, he looked pleased as punch.

But as soon as his height betrayed his approach to Ethel's grave-projector, suddenly Ethel appeared and the first time it occurred that he was no longer in his good books, was when he heart the sharp tone of his darling wife, and what gave away his sudden predicament of finding himself immersed in her wrath was when his ear heard the piercing, "ARTHUR TRUFFLES, YOU HAVE SOME GALL TURNING UP HERE WITH A MEETING OF YOUR WIFE, DRIVING A CAR WHICH YOU ACTUALLY SPENT £ 30,000 OF MY HARD-EARNED MONEY ON!"

All Arthur could do was gulp, as in "GULP!"

"ARTHUR TRUFFLES, IN EXCHANGE FOR £30,000 YOU HAVE A TOY FOR A TOY-BOY'S CAR!" Ethel boomed in fury.

Arthur gulped again and his natural instincts was to take a U-turn and retreat back to his Jaguar than rather suffer her wrath, stinging rebuke if his wife, which he felt was in real life, and he felt she was so close and speaking to him there and then that he felt so defensive of his physical safety from her wrath, that he instinctively turned around to go back to his car and drive back home; if she had resorted to whacking him with one of her saucepans, he would think that it would be physically painful for him, such was the effectiveness of these second generation or Holograms called Holygram Mark Two.

So after a time, these holograms started becoming more and more a source of not comfort but rather something of an intrusion and source of irritation. At first they were a great source of comfort for Arthur, especially in cushioning the shock and sudden departure of his dearly beloved wife.

But after some time, Arthur felt that his wife was breathing down his neck, constantly watching his every move. Arthur was now beginning to find that technology very intrusive.

And Arthur was beginning to think that it was high-time he took a holiday from all the stress of recent weeks – what with having to deal with the sudden loss of being forced to bury and come to terms with the sudden death of his wife of forty-five years, and then the new and demanding responsibilities of looking after his twin-sons who were almost almost grown up, who he planned to bring along with him on his 'hols'.

So Arthur decided it was a hightime he took a holiday with his boys, to relax a bit and have quality time with them. And whether they wanted to come or not, he had determined to go for a holiday to either the Algarve or Antigua. And that was one reason why he paid Ethel another visit to ask her opinion of which destination to go to, either Portugal or Spain.

"Yes, I think I've earned a trip abroad." He thought to himself as he rocked his favorite chair, his own rocking chair, which helped him to counter his daily intakes of stress and digest everything he had taken that day.

"But when Ethel got wind of his intention, she thought that instead of spending his money, now was the time, he should be thrifty and save, especially for their two sons, Tommy and Peter.

So the next time Arthur visited her graveside, she gave him such an ear-bashing, he instead took a two week break to Torquay or Torbay – which was a compromise after ditching his plans of holidaying in the Algarve or Antigua. Arthur was sitting in front of Ethel's grave – he had, as he does these days, carried his own personal rocking chair to sit and chat with Ethel. And Arthur just started to chat how much he would have liked Ethel to come along with him on his trip to either Antigia or the Algarve – actually he wanted to use Ethel as a sounding board to help him decide which destination was best:

"So Ethel I was thinking, where would you have preferred to go to - Antigua or the Algarve?"

"Oh, Ethel, these days, I'm planning a little trip abroad and I would so wish that you could have come along and joined me as well. Just like old-times, eh, Ethel, my Honeypot!"

The End of Part One, Please Watch for Part Two.

9 781006 788222